Praise for Extinction Journals
& Jeremy Robert Johnson

"DUCK AND COVER, BITCHES! Jeremy Robert Johnson answers the call to glory with his intimately insectoid mini-epic of apocalypse, *Extinction Journals*: a trip far weirder and more fucked up than it has any right to be. Just like these times."
- John Skipp, author of *Conscience*, co-author/editor of *The Scream, Mondo Zombie*, and *Book of the Dead*

"*Extinction Journals* is like a Twilight Zone episode made without Standards & Practices telling Serling he couldn't feature any human/insect love scenes. Move over Chris Genoa-there's a new sexy genius in town."
- Chris Genoa, author of *Foop!*

"Johnson swirls just enough lucidity and knowing, zombie-Vonnegut hilarity into his bizarro fable of mutually assured delirium to make me question my own sanity. Until science finds a cure for whatever ails this boy, we can only hope to bask in the cool plutonium glow of his weaponized mind... and start collecting cockroaches."
- Cody Goodfellow, author of *Radiant Dawn* and *Ravenous Dusk*

EXTINCTION JOURNALS

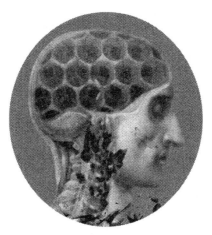

Jeremy Robert Johnson

Swallowdown Press
Portland, OR

ISBN: 1-933929-01-4

Library of Congress Control Number: 2006902930

Swallowdown Press
PO Box 2466
Portland, OR 97208-2466
U.S.A.

Book Design by Carlton Mellick III

Printed in the United States of America

Dedication

To Chuck Palahniuk, Steve Vernon, Jackson Ellis, Tom Piccirilli, and Girl on Demand at POD-dy Mouth- five very kind people who convinced others I had stories worth hearing.

Acknowledgements

Further thanks are due to Carlton Mellick III and Mitch Maraude (for throwing down the gauntlet), to Chris, Cody, and John (for reading this bugger and finding something nice to say about it), and to Jessica (for everything, always).

Extinction Journals

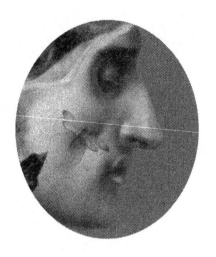

Chapter One

The cockroaches took several hours to eat the President. That much Dean was sure of. His buggy business suit had a severe appetite. Anything else- life/reality/desire- came across secondary and suspect. Although Dean *was* fairly positive that World War III had begun. Extent of the carnage- Unknown. Nations involved- Unknown. Survivors he was aware of- One.

There were two, originally. The President *had* been alive when Dean found him out here by the base of the Washington Monument. The guy was nearly catatonic, pacing a small circle, slack-jawed, but breathing. Still, he never had a chance. When a man in a suit made of cockroaches meets a man in a suit made of Twinkies- well, that's about as easy as subtraction gets.

As scenarios go, Dean branded this one Capital L Lonely. He'd choked out the President as an act of mercy, to save the man the sensation of being eaten alive. That meant that at present Dean had not a soul to talk to.

He tried to address the suit.

"Hey, roaches. Are you guys full yet?"

Nothing. Or maybe they thought it rude to respond while eating.

Instead, Dean's Fear, that nagging voice that he thought he'd snuffed out by surviving the bombing, decided to chip in.

Yeah, that's reasonable. Talk to the insects. How cracked is your mind at this point? Are you even sure you're alive? I mean, we're talking full-fledged nuclear war here. You absolutely should not be alive. It's ridiculous. How do you know that you weren't vaporized in the first blast? That's more likely. And this is some sort of nasty purgatory that you'll be forever condemned to, all alone, stuck in this ugly place with your ludicrous bug suit...

"Shut up." It felt better to Dean, saying it out loud. Quieted the ugly part of his brain for a moment at least.

Dean was pretty sure that he was alive. He couldn't imagine a metaphysical plane where he'd feel so damn hungry.

I need to pee. There's no way they kept urination in the afterlife.

Dean was also pretty sure that the world, or at least his continent, was getting darker and heading towards deep-sea black. It was already beyond dusk at what was probably three in the afternoon. Nuclear winter was spreading its ashy chill through the air, fed onward by black smoke and blazing nouveau-palace pyres in the distance. Fat flakes of glowing grey floated in the air.

Dean shivered and tried to move the heft of his weight into the radiant heat coming from the bodies of the cockroaches beneath him. There were tiny pores in the suit's fabric at each point where he'd delicately sewn each roach's thorax to the outfit. He imagined heat seeping through, but didn't really feel it.

Dean received little comfort or consolation. But he didn't demand those things either. The suit kept him alive here at catastrophe central and Dean felt guilty for wanting more.

Relax. Let the suit take the lead. Let instinct kick in. They've had millions of years of training. They're ready for this.

But why are they eating so much? They never needed this much food before.

Dean blanched. This level of consumption was totally un-natural. He'd guessed they'd stop feeding when they finished with the toasted yellow sugar cakes the President had been coated in.

Back when Dean had lived in the slums of DC, as he was creating the suit, he'd woken many evenings and found the creatures nibbling at the dead skin around his eyelashes and fingernails, but he'd never seen them go after new, wet meat like this. What, he wondered, had he strapped onto his body?

Maybe they'll turn right around when they're done with El Presidente here and they'll keep on eating. Could you fight them off Dean? The leader of the free world couldn't stop them. What makes you think you could? You think these roaches know you? That they give a petty shit about you and your continued existence? They're filling up Dean. They'll eat you slow...

"Fuck that fuck that fuck that." Dean had to say this out loud, and quickly, to clear his mental slate. With nowhere to go the Fear could run rampant if he didn't run containment. The rolling sheet of hunger Dean had clothed himself inside of just kept eating. It took in a million tiny bits of once stately matter and processed President in its guts.

Could they taste the man's power, Dean wondered, like an Iroquois swallowing his enemy's heart? A fool's question, but he had little to do but think and adjust while his handcrafted cockroach suit stayed true to its sole purpose- Survival.

Here, amid the ash of the freshly destroyed capital, hunkered over an ever-thinner corpse in the shadow of a blackened obelisk, Dean's suit was fueling up for potential famine/war/voyage. The legion of bugs sewn into the front of his suit jacket and pants clung tight to the supine body of the recently deceased world leader, forcing Dean into a sort of lover's embrace with a man he'd once feared and despised more than any other. And there were so many mouths to feed. A multitude of mandibles denuding bone, sucking skin off of the fingers that had presumably launched the first volley of nuclear arsenal earlier that day. Cockroach jaws chewing away at the kingly lips which had once taunted foreign dignitaries and charmed the breadbasket into submission with phrase like, "HOO BOY, and good morning to you!"

Despite the largely unappetizing sounds of insect consumption beneath him, Dean felt a low grumble in his own gut.

Will they let me eat? Do they have to get their fill before I can find something for myself?

He pushed down on the cold, dirty ground with his

bare hands, again regretting his oversight during the design phase. His cockroach suit, completed with the addition of blast goggles, an oxygen tank and mask, a skull-topper crash helmet, and foil-lined tan work boots, was totally lacking the crucial support that a pair of nice woolly gloves could provide. Dean cursed himself and pictured surging blast rads sneaking into his heart via his exposed fingertips. He felt gamma ray death in the grit beneath his tightly-groomed nails.

You won't make it a day, Dean-o. You're probably dead anyway, right? This is your hell, Dean. You'll be here, right here, forever. You'll keep getting hungrier and hungrier while the radiation makes you puke your guts out and you'll feel every...last...second...

"Quiet!"

Dean shifted his legs against the tugging movements of the roaches on their prey and managed to get the toes of his boots planted firmly behind him. Now all he had to do was push up and away from the ground and hope he could break the masticating grip of the ravenous bugs sewn to his suit.

Jaw clenched tight/teeth squeaking with stress/thin muscles pumping at max output. Still, no give. The thick cloister of bugs that covered Dean's chest had dug deep into the corpse. Dean could tell from the stink of half-digested lobster bisque that the bugs had breached the President's belly. Worse, the smell only made him hungrier.

Cannibal. Beast.

"Shut it shut it shut it."

Dean readied himself again, flattening his hands, fingers wide, anxious to assert his own need to survive. He and the roaches had to learn to live *together.* If not in total symbiosis, then through equal shows of force- a delicate balance between Dean and his meticulously crafted attire.

They'd be a team, damn it.

Dean pushed, exhaling sharply, goggles fogging up with exertion, sweat pooling at his lower back.

Come on. We can take the body with us. I just need to get some food in my belly and you greedy little fuckers can return to your meal. Just let go...

Dean pushed and felt a shift. He realized that his full-force push-up had only served to elevate him *and* the body stuck to him, just before he realized his shaking right hand was edging into a patch of blood-spattered Twinkie filling.

Quick as a thought Dean's hand slid out from under his newly acquired girth, and he thudded back to the ground. The weight of the landing was enough to compress a stale breath through the lungs of the President's body.

And Dean would swear, to his last day, that the impact of his weight on the President's chest forced a final "HOO BOY!" from the dead man's half-eaten lips.

It was upon hearing this final and desperate State of the Union Address that Dean allowed exhaustion, un-sated hunger and shock to overcome him.

He rested deeply, cradled by a suit that slept in shifts and fed each of its members a royal feast.

This was the first day of the end of human existence.

Chapter Two

Deep belly grumbles/acidic clenching. The light pain of an oncoming hunger headache made mostly unimportant by the stranger sensation of being in motion while in the process of waking.

Dean opened his eyes and rubbed accumulated ash from his blast goggles. The suit was moving, quickly, away from something. He couldn't shake the God-like sensation he got when the roaches carried him across the ground.

Overlord Dean. The Great One To Which We Cling. The Mighty Passenger.

Dean would have been more amused by his invented titles had he not noticed what the suit was fleeing from.

A thick bank of radioactive fog was rolling in behind them, moving in the new alien currents created by a global weather system blown topsy-turvy. It had a reddish tint at its edges that read cancer/mutation/organ-sloughing. Dean imagined each of the nuclear droplets must be nearly frozen inside the fog. The temperature was cold enough to sap the heat from his fingers and face. Thirty-five degrees and dropping, easy.

But the roaches could handle the sort of deep level radiation that filled the fog. Were they moving in order to try and preserve *him*? Ridiculous. So they must have exhausted their food source and were just moving towards the next step. A dark place to hide. A place to nestle in and lay eggs.

Should I just let them keep leading me along? The way they'd treated their last meal... if I don't take over now they'll never let me eat. They'll just keep moving and consuming. Hell, with it this dark outside, they won't even feel a need to hide. This is their world now. I've got to show them I deserve a place in it.

Carefully, so as not to crush any of the suit's communal members, he lowered his heels to the ground and then got his feet beneath him. Within seconds he was standing, lightheaded and waiting for the blood to catch up. The few Madagascar cockroaches he'd sown to his pants, amid all the Germans and Smokybrowns, jostled at the disturbance and let loose with high-pitched hissing.

"Come on you guys. Take it easy."

Dean ignored their susurrant complaint. He respected the suit, but now it was time for the suit to respect him. He felt the roaches' legs bicycling in the chill wind, seeking purchase, trying to stay on target with wherever they'd been headed.

Maybe I should let them take over. They got me through the overpressure of the blast. They got me through the radiation, so far. They found food instantly in a dead landscape. They're almost happy, it seems. Vibrating. Thriving. Do I have that same instinct?

I have to. No choice. Assess the situation.

Dean ignored the motions of his suit, took a few breaths from his oxygen mask to try and clear the chemical taste from his throat, and realized that he really should have hooked up a gas mask instead of his portable breather unit.

But he couldn't subject himself to that level of suffering. Dean had a severe aversion to having his entire face enclosed in rubber; an extraordinarily rough time with a dominatrix in Iceland had forced him to forever swear off such devices. He could barely even tolerate the tiny respirator.

Now, though, he couldn't help wonder about what this tainted air was already doing to his lungs. And he thanked the collective gods for whatever miracle had prevented the small oxygen tank on his back from exploding when the first bomb sent out its terrible heat-wave.

I can't fucking believe I'm still alive.

It was quickly becoming a mantra, but a useless one which distracted him from the act of actually living.

He shook away the thought, surveyed his surroundings.

Black rubble. Fire. Ash. Nothing remotely human or animal in any direction. Whatever bombs were employed- fission/fusion/gun-triggered/dirty bombs/H-bombs- they did the job to the Nth degree. The view triggered Fear.

Last man standing, Dean-o. Look at the world you've inherited. All the nothing you could ever want. You're either stuck in this till the end of time or…

"Enough. No."

It was night-time. Maybe. Or the sky born debris had completely blocked out the sunlight. Regardless, still-flaming buildings were the remaining source of illumination. Dean figured anything that depended on photosynthesis was torched or starving at top speed in the blackout.

He couldn't assess his distance from the ground zero hypocenter but he guessed he was within fifty miles of an actual strike.

That's good, Dean. Pretend you know what's going on. Pretend you aren't a man coated in cockroaches and that you can make sense of the world. But remember that if the world makes sense, you're dead. Are you dead?

The black clouds above rolled over each other with super-natural momentum, colliding and setting off electrical storms that flashed wide but never struck the ground. There were few high points left to arc through.

Dean felt strangely honored as a witness. For all he knew, his were the last human eyes taking in a vision that royally outranked Mt. St. Helens or Pinatubo, and surely even went beyond what the first people to emerge from tunnel shelters at Nagasaki saw.

Don't drift. Think. Take action.

He ran down research, looking for a plan. He spoke the details aloud to his suit, and hoped that somehow they were paying attention. Teamwork would remain crucial.

"Okay, guys, here's what we're looking at. Assuming bombs haven't hit every single inch of the U.S., we might be able to clear the fallout ground track by heading out 30 miles past the central explosion. Rain and fog this close to the blast will jack the fallout up to intolerable levels. If we can find a safe place for now, and hole up for three to five weeks, then our travel options should open wide. The radiation will drop by then. Decontamination requires things we don't have-flowing water/backhoes/man-power. We're going to have to soak up some rads no matter what. Not that you guys are worried about that."

No response.

Were you expecting one, Dean-o? Are you that gone?

But Dean didn't expect any response. What he didn't tell his Fear, what he didn't want to say or even think, really, was that the loneliness was already making him feel sad in a way that was dangerous. Dean had never spent much time talking to people in the months just prior, but there'd been some interaction each day. The mailman. Fast food clerks. Small vestiges of human interaction. Faces that reacted. Voices that weren't his.

Dean continued to lay out the game plan.

"We can access emergency drinking water by filtering contaminated H20 through more than ten inches of dirt. But that dirt had better be from below the topsoil, which is toxic in and of itself right now. Access to a supply of potassium iodide could mitigate some of the effects of the radiation on me, not that you guys care about that."

He almost hoped for a response to that last part. Some sign from the roaches that they did indeed give a shit. But there was nothing.

"The top new symptoms on my watch list will be nausea, vomiting, diarrhea, cataracts, and hair loss."

Of course, Dean's constant exposure to the cockroaches and their profusion of pathogens meant he was often riddled with the first three symptoms, but if they got much worse than usual....

And what about the suit itself? Dean decided to skip talking to them about these details.

He'd expected the roaches sewn to him- at least the females- to survive for two hundred days or so. As long as they had food and water they'd get by. Perhaps, within that time span, the Earth would find some new equilibrium in its atmosphere and Dean could survive without his living fabric.

What the hell kind of plan is that? Did I even believe, deep down, that this suit would have actually kept me alive? Maybe it was just something to do to keep the Fear away until I died. Like old folks playing bridge.

No. Somehow I knew this would work.

And I lived. I'm living. Now I have to keep things that way.

Dean wasn't sure how to feel about the ever-worsening nuclear winter growling around him. He dropped the roach edification because he was a bit confused on the whole issue.

Best I only speak to them in a confident tone, or not at all.

Back in the Seventies nuclear winter had been declared humankind's endgame by Sagan and the Soviets. But in the Eighties Thompson and Schneider played that off as Cold War propaganda. So the weather was either headed towards the colder and darker spectrum, or was hitting its worst and soon to wane. Better to error on the side of Sagan and hook up some Arctic gear in case the temperature went negative. Easier to strip that stuff off if it turned out that the long-lasting dinosaur-and-human-ending nuclear winter was just a big Russian bluff.

Food. Dean's main mission until his belly became quiet, and something he figured his pals would like to hear about.

"Listen up, guys. Assuming not *everything* was vaporized, there should be enough in warehouses and stocks to feed the entire U.S. for sixty to ninety days. The rest of the world will be worse off. Maybe thirty three days of food before they run out." *And will they be able to get to the U.S. at that point? Would they be coming for your food, Dean, those starving pirate citizens from small countries deemed Not Worth Bombing but still dependent on the global infrastructure for grub?*

He shook off the doubts and tried to inject his voice with renewed poise.

"What about cows? There should be cows around. Somewhere. A non-irradiated bovine could supply us with food, milk or even an extra layer of leather protection."

Not, Dean realized, that he would know how the hell to go about starting that process. He'd never touched a cow that wasn't already sectioned and shrink-wrapped.

There was never enough time to learn the tools needed for surviving the apocalypse. Too many ways for a planet to go rotten.

Dean laid out a plan. And as plans go, it was on the lackluster end of things. The problem- he'd spent so much time thinking and chatting up the roaches that his hunger had crept full force into his brain.

Now all he and his belly could coherently put together was the following:

Get Food.

Dean asserted himself. He trekked on foot, away from the blast center and the noxious red fog bank that seemed to keep rolling inland. His fingers went numb. He wished he hadn't sewn the pockets shut on his jacket and pants, but had needed to in order to ensure every inch of his outfit was roach-ready.

His headache pushed inward, its own fog rolling

through the crags of his cerebellum.

He cursed the extra weight of the oxygen tank on his back. He junked it.

He'd adapt to the new air like he'd adapted to the roaches. He'd press his limits. Couldn't stomach that mask anyway. It conjured up flashes of too-long ball-gagged seconds at the hands of his Icelandic ex-mistress. The smell of vomit trapped between skin and rubber. A pressure behind the eyes.

His mouth tasted of the burning tenements that flanked him, of dried cat shit under a sun-lamp. He knew he was wasted if his thirst outgrew his hunger.

Water. Food. Now.

No one to talk to. Nothing to see but burning buildings, gutted cracking skeleton structures that might once have held sustenance.

Depression hit quick, ran through Dean's whole body like a low-grade fever that only served to slow him further as he slogged onward.

So. You lived. What now? Why keep going? Daddy Dean Sr.'s money doesn't matter any more, you little trust fund bitch. You don't really know how to survive. What were the odds your numb-nuts roach suit experiment would have worked? Why do you deserve to keep going when millions just died? You manage to survive a nuclear blast, and kill the President, the man you thought had a personal hard-on for your death. In one day you conquered both your greatest fears. Victory was yours, right? And now you'll die because you didn't think to pack a loaf of bread and some bottled water in that suit. You're letting a bunch of shit-sucking insects dictate the flow of your life.

Shall I go on?

Water. All Dean wanted was some water. He was cold, but if he stepped closer to the smoldering buildings his lips cracked and his thirst grew. It was a head-fucker. *You don't have any reasons to stay alive. The man who kept you going- the man who gave you something to fight against- is turning into plastered pellets of roach shit all around you. What are you going to do? Find a woman? Re-populate the Earth? You never really liked people before. Empathized maybe, but never really felt any communal love. Women wouldn't talk to you before, Dean. You think you'll be a big charmer now, Roach Man?*

One foot in front of the other. Twelve slow, slogging miles. The edge of the city. What *was* the city. What would now be referred to euphemistically as a "site."

There- the empty field that bordered the suburban intersection. A small tin shed. Not black. Not burning.

You'll be like them soon. The roaches. Just living. Thoughtless. You'll be sterilized. Your guts will blacken. The end of you. But they'll breed. They'll keep going. And you'll be dragged with them to the end, shoving carrion and rotten plants into your mouth if they'll let you.

Finally, a vision. Might be an oasis.

Dean stumbled forward and gently crouched before the shapes that leaned against the western side of the building. The nagging voice in his head fell away as he bent down beside the tiny metal shed and picked up the sealed jar of water and single pre-packed cup of chocolate pudding.

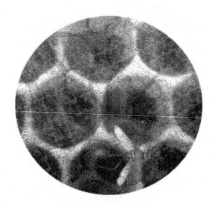

Chapter Three

Pudding beats sex, big time. Of course, having had little sex, most of it running the gamut from earnest/mediocre to awkward/ugly, Dean found this comparison easy to make.

He tried to eat slow, to let the tiny chocolate heavens loll on his tongue before gulping the gel down, but it wasn't easy.

It's just so...goddamned...GOOD!

He nearly choked on a runny cocoa dollop when he tried to pull a breath through his nose while swallowing. But he held the cough. Kept the pudding in his mouth. Every little drop of it. He licked the last bits from his unwashed fingers and ushered untold levels of bacteria into his gut. He knew it. He just couldn't stop himself.

Then he had to rinse it down.

Get some water in my system. Get my head on straight.

The Fear seemed to be gone, chased away by sugar

to the brain and Dean's new sense that he was truly alive and breathing.

Somehow I'm... here.

He unscrewed the lid of the Mason jar, which gave a satisfying pop as its seal ruptured. He already had three quarters of the pudding-tinted water down his throat before he remembered.

Shit. They need water too.

Dean hesitated. Felt the water rushing through his body, his headache already distant. Those terrible voices quieted. He thought about how much better he'd feel with the rest of that water running down his gullet. Thought about how the suit had denied him even a hint of food when it had access.

No, that's not right. Maybe if I give them water now, they'll learn. They didn't survive this many years without being able to quickly adapt to new scenarios. Maybe I can establish trust.

As silly as the thought felt in his head, it also had a weird ring of truth. Lions and hyenas learned to share in their own brutal environment. Maybe even the bug's cutthroat existence didn't have to be all or nothing.

Dean realized that hand feeding was not an option. To find a way to apply water to each of those tiny mouths would be ridiculous even if he had the time/energy/patience. This was never a problem before. The suit had always fed solo, safely stored within a lock-box in Dean's rat-trap apartment. He wasn't sure how to hydrate them in the present since he didn't dare remove the outfit. They were absorbing who knows how much radiation right now, shielding Dean's fragile skin and organs from invisible rays.

How would they get the water if I wasn't here?

With that thought, Dean walked into the small hollow tin structure and gently poured the remaining water out on the concrete floor. Luckily it was poorly laid and the water puddled at a concavity in the center of the cement.

Dean eased himself onto the ground, lying prone.

"Drink up, little guys."

They took to it like pros, the most robust sections of the suit contorting to the puddle first and siphoning up their own tiny portions of liquid life.

Dean's right arm was drinking from the pool. He peered upward at the ramshackle lid on the structure and noticed that it was starting to lift up, as if a wind was catching beneath it. The hairs on his neck popped rigid.

The shack's lid raised and slapped back down twice, shaking the whole building. Then it simply disappeared. No tearing away at creaky hinges and rusty nails. The thing was just *gone*. Dean's skin ran wild over spasming muscles.

Another blast? A second volley? Who was left to launch this one? Was New Zealand armed? Did the Maoris have missiles, half-etched with tribal paint, striking down on U.S. soil?

No. There was no heat this time. No terrible pressure.

The roaches had stopped drinking. They began to crawl, frantically, out of the shed and into the open field. They did circles, unsure of where to go, Dean riding their agitated wave.

Dean had seen this type of motion in roaches before, prior to figuring out how to rig his apartment with UV lights. The bugs were steeped in negative phototropism, it was a key to their continued existence. Allowed them to function out of sight of their predators.

And what they were doing now was exactly what they used to do when he'd arrive home and switch on the overhead lamps.

But where was the light coming from? All Dean could see was the steady wavering light of fires succumbing to the increasing chill of nuclear winter.

Dean pushed off of the ground and stood up, halting the flight of the cockroaches against his better judgment. He had to figure out what they were running from. What if it was an airplane? Something else? Another survivor?

Dean craned his neck and pushed his blast goggles up into his hairline to make sure he could see as well as possible.

It was then that Dean's pupils began to fluctuate in size and his stomach threatened to surrender its precious pudding.

Because, as Dean looked skyward, he saw a great chariot of fire and aboard that chariot, the shape of something like a man.

Trumpets sounded, a terrible multitude of them, a great shrieking air raid that threatened to cave Dean's eardrums had he not shielded them with chocolate-streaked hands.

The chariot, and the shape it carried, were headed straight for him. Bearing down at top-speed. The figure in the chariot was definitely humanoid, with a head, two arms, and a torso, but the skin shimmered with silver and hints of the full spectrum. The thing had but one great eye at the center of its head.

Dean felt no heat from the chariot but noted that the roaches coating him were frantically trying to escape to anywhere, to be free of that brilliant light.

Then the chariot halted, perhaps fifty feet from where

Dean stood with his mouth agape.

Then the chariot just disappeared. Gone. Poof. Like the top of the tin shed.

That was when Dean decided to turn and run. Anything that can make matter disappear- majestic though it may be- was dangerous.

"HALT!"

Dean halted. That *voice*- part insect/part trumpet/part his father's.

He turned to face the creature.

It hovered there for a moment, where its burning chariot had stood, and then floated slowly towards the ground before Dean.

Dean nearly lost his legs. His teeth squeaked against each other. Sweat popped along his forehead. But he stood strong- falling now meant the roaches would continue their frantic escape.

The shape landed just three feet from Dean, and though it didn't radiate heat, Dean suspected that the ground beneath the thing would have ignited had it not already been charred clean.

Thunder rolled in the purple/black clouds above them.

The thing stared through Dean with its one huge eye.

Dean surveyed the creature. It returned the same. From what Dean was seeing he could think of only a few words.

Ergot. Mycotoxin.

Whatever was in that pudding, it's driven me mad. Is there grain in pudding? Could it go bad all sealed up like that? Was the pudding full of gamma rays?

Have I finally snapped?

He remembered the rough times after his father had

passed away in a brutal deer/Slurpee straw/airbag-related auto accident. Dean had chased a new life then, thought he could find it through drugs and rituals and chants and smoke ceremonies. Instead he'd only found Fear, the same cold gut feeling that had inspired him to build his cockroach suit.

But in all his travels, all those long nights of the soul, chasing demons on the dirt floor of some shaman's hut, he'd never seen anything this wondrous.

The creature stood at the same height as Dean, the exact same, although this felt like an illusion to induce comfort. It had the limbs of a human, although Dean could perceive no joints. It appeared, in fact, to be liquid, with a skin of entirely separated translucent scales floating over the shifting eddies and rivers and storming oceans of its surface. Each scale cycled through the spectrum, every color that Dean's eyes could perceive. He felt as if his brain was learning to interpret new shades with each second, colors without names. A painter, Dean thought, would be in tears right now.

At the center of the thing's chest a thin pink light shone through the scales as they whirled from torso to limb to face to back.

The great eye regarded Dean without any clear emotion. Human facial expressions would, Dean knew, appear petty across this surface.

The thing emitted a low, nearly sub-sonic noise and the roach suit seemed to dive into a comatose state. The feelers and legs stopped their incessant clawing at the air.

Eight long tendrils of light unfurled from the creature's back, straightening themselves out in direct opposition of each other, their points forming a perfect circle behind it.

Dean had been without God, without wonder, for years since Daddy Dean Sr. had passed, but he was about to weep when the creature spoke. It had no mouth. Rather, the voice, *that voice*, appeared directly in Dean's head asking: "Where did everybody go?"

Dean was unsure how to respond, or if he even should. Was this a test? What revelations were about to occur? "Where did everybody go?" The creature wanted a response. But surely something this wondrous would already know the answer. "No. I don't know what's going on. Something has changed. Today was supposed to be the time of my manifestation."

"Your manifestation? I'm sorry, I'm just so..."

"You don't have to use your mouth to communicate right now. I can speak inside of your mind, but cannot see through it as much as I need to. Please open it up to me. I'm going to emit a frequency, and once you do the same, we'll have an open line."

Dean had no idea how to "emit a frequency" but the creature began to vibrate and a low humming noise came from its center. It rattled through Dean's bones and he found himself humming until his throat was producing the same tone.

"There" the thing said, "We're in line with each other now. I can tell from your colors that you are confused. So much grey."

Dean had experienced the hucksterism of aura reading before. He began to think of ergotism and bad pudding again. Nothing was making sense.

"I can help you," said the thing. "First, I'll share my wisdom, then I'll ask for yours. Does this sound okay?"

Dean nodded Yes inside of his head and kept humming.

A thin purple lid dropped over the creature's color-shifting eye and it began to tremble. A lower hum rattled through Dean's ribcage, and he feared his heart might collapse. The pressure continued to build and then there was a thumping sound and the creature's knowledge came pouring into Dean's mind. Dean struggled against the flow and tried to hum back questions when he was lost.

"The creatures of this planet have called me down to unite them. They have abandoned their earliest forms of energy transmittal, what some call religion. The disparate forms of energy they've since adapted and harnessed have fractured the colors that float around their sphere."

"Sphere. You mean Earth?"

"Yes, you could call it that. These new energy systems ran thick with dark currents and were quickly poisoned. Even once noble ideas collapsed under structure and hierarchy and the presence of the human identity. Possession. Power. Control. Life was bridled. The focus was shifted towards the individual bits of matter that made up this sphere."

"Bits of matter. You mean the living things."

"Sort of. But most of those things stayed pure. The parts of the sphere that called themselves 'I' were the source of the poison. But something inside their replicative code recognized the sickness and began to create me."

"So humankind's DNA recognized that religious systems were pulling the species further and further away from some lifeforce that drives our existence?"

"Well, sort of. How much do you know about super-strings? Whorls? Vortex derivatives?"

"Oh, god, nothing at all."

"Okay, that doesn't help. Is there someone else around here that I can talk to? This is much easier if I can speak in your mathematics. I mean, I know you people understand this. All I am is a gradually amassed energy force that your being created. I don't exist beyond the scope of the power that already runs through your body."

"My body?"

"Yes, your body. The infinite spaces in between the atoms that compose you, and the matter itself."

"I'm really lost now. Are you sure you're making sense? Maybe we're humming at different frequencies or something... hold up... no that hum sounds about right. Listen, I've had a really rough day and I think maybe I got a hold of some bad pudding and I'm hoping you can just amplify your powers and give me all this knowledge at once, in a way that encapsulates it so that I fully understand."

"That's not how it works. Unearned realization does nothing to shift the colors. There were supposed to be billions of you when I arrived. The collective unconscious would have ignited, all religions would have fallen. Time as you know it would have ceased its passage and all human matter would have lost its identity and returned to its source, where a new lifeform would have been created, one properly coded for continued existence and evolution."

"The Rapture?"

"We were going to allow you to call it that. Your belief gave that concept power. And all the energy systems, even those that did not espouse it, found the idea enchanting, so it would have been very effective. Those with the slightest vibration of the old energy at their core would have floated up and merged with me, bathed in my energy. Any others would have softly ceased to exist, floating away in a warm surge of white light."

"So what now?"

"Exactly. I'm lost. I exist, and am present, so something of the old belief must still exist. Something on this sphere, other than you, is alive and believes that I should be."

"So, are you going to wash me away in soft light now?"

"No. Everything has changed. I must adapt. Which means I need your help. Please tell me, *where did everybody go?*"

"They're dead. All of them, so far as I know. The President was still alive a while ago, but my suit ate him. It's really hard to explain."

"I have nowhere else to go. Neither do you. You may have noticed I've halted time."

Dean had wondered why the roaches were so still.

"Okay. I'll give it a shot."

Dean let loose what he knew through a series of modulated hums. He waxed as poetic as he could about the Cold War, the Iraq wars, Sierra Leone, the fall of Russia, nuclear proliferation, his country's tyrannical hillbilly puppet leader, Wal-Mart, peak oil, the internet, pandemics, suburban sprawl, the ultimate fallibility of the President's Twinkie suit (although Dean admired it in theory), colonialism, plastics, uranium, fast food, and global conflict. But when he got to the end of the story it felt like the whole thing was a colossal waste of time because the punchline, no matter what, was this:

…and then we killed ourselves.

Which, Dean felt, was a terribly down way to end his story.

The creature agreed. It shook its beautiful mono-orbital head and retracted the long whips of light that had extended from its back.

"So what" Dean asked, "are you going to do now?"

"I'm not sure. Without your species, I doubt I'll exist

much longer. I'll probably just fade back into the ether. The worst part is, I think I know why I was finally called down, why the energy was strong enough to bring about a change."

"Will I understand it if you tell me?"

"Probably. When the bombs started dropping, I think people forgot all of the dark systems that might once have ruled over them. And I think, for a moment, they found their way back into the old energies."

"You mean they were all praying before they died?"

"Not exactly. Sort of. It's not really prayer. It's this state the mind goes into when it knows it's about to die. There's a lot of power there."

"But it was too late?"

"From what you've told me, yes."

"Shit…"

Time must have started to flow again. Dean felt the bite of hot tears in his eyes.

"Does that make you sad?"

"I guess. I get this feeling when I think about people dying. Mostly, I just feel bad that *they're* so sad about it happening. And that sadness is strong. I'm afraid of it. So what I do is ignore them and just focus on staying alive. Because as long as I'm here, as long as I'm living and fighting off death, then I feel alright…I don't ever want to feel as sad as those people."

"But death is natural. It's part of how your particular energy stays in existence."

"Yeah, people always say that, but lions eating people is natural, too, and I'd chew my way through a room full of boiled shit to avoid ever ending up in the jaws of some giant cat, even for a second."

"You still don't understand."

"No, you don't understand. I'm here and I'm *alive* and that's the one thing I've ever known for sure since I started breathing. I understand just fine."

The creature sighed, and began to turn.

"You're going then?"

"Of course. No reason to stay here. You're dead already."

"Oh, c'mon. Don't be like that. Maybe I can learn from you. Will you at least tell me your name?"

"Had I needed a name during my time here, you would have called me Yahmuhwesu."

"That's a terrible name."

"I thought so, too. It's not my fault you've got an ugly language. But it would have worked. The floating horseless fire chariot wasn't my idea either. But according to the vibrations from the hive mind, it would have been the most impressive way to appear."

"Probably. Can I ask where you're going?"

"Sure. I can still feel a pull here, so I'm going to look for other humans. If I find another, perhaps something will come of it. If not...."

"Well then, Yahmuhwesu, goodbye. Wish me luck."

"Despite knowing better, I will."

His feet lifted from the black floor of the Earth, floating just inches above it.

"And by the way, Dean, I thought you might find this amusing. For a man with such a singular obsession with death, you are *hugely* pregnant."

Chapter Four

Pudding doesn't taste as good on the way back up.

Dean noted this as he wiped a string of bilious choco-late drool from his lower lip and surveyed the sad pool of snack treat that sat beneath him in the charred soil.

Pregnant? What the hell is he talking about? You can't just tell a man he's pregnant and then disappear from existence like that. It's too much.

Dean couldn't fathom the idea of licking up the pud-ding off the ground, so he eased himself into a supine position and let the suit have at it. They deserved a little sugar. God knows what being frozen in time did to the poor things.

Dean's body rotated slowly over the ground as the roaches took turns feeding on the regurgitated confection.

I hope they hurry up. We need to keep moving inland.

It had to be a coincidence, but as Dean had the thought he felt the bugs beneath him pick up their pace, shuffling quicker through their arcane feeding system.

Weird. I must be in shock. First I'm talking to some sort of scaly god, now I'm imagining that roaches can read my mind.

Pregnant. What could that have meant?

Then Dean realized what Yahmuhwesu was talking about.

The roaches. They'd been attached to the suit for a few weeks now. Long enough for some of them to reproduce. Especially the German ones. They didn't even need sex to breed.

When choosing the different types of roaches for his suit, Dean had put them through a rigorous series of survival tests. The Smokybrowns and Orientals had done well, extraordinary paragons of genetics really. But the Blatella germanica was in a class of its own.

He'd cut the head off of a German and watched it navigate through tubes back to its preferred spot by the baseboard molding in the corner of his bathroom.

Then he took the headless roach and put it in an airtight jar so see how long it would keep going. Ten days later the decapitated juggernaut was not only in motion, but had sprouted an egg case from its abdomen.

A week later there were thirty nymphs in the jar. They looked healthy. And full, since they'd eaten their headless mother.

Right then Dean had made the choice. His suit was going to be seventy percent German. It upped his odds. You just couldn't kill the damn things.

Dean slid his goggles down and cleared them of deposited ash. He tilted his head forward. He lifted his right arm off of the ground, anxious to see if any of his roaches were reproducing.

Yahmuhwesu was right. Dean wasn't just pregnant, he was completely covered in life. An egg case for almost every German. Even the ones he could have sworn were male a week ago.

Shit. That's a lot of extra mouths to feed.

Dean gave himself a week, maybe two before they hatched.

And what if they think of you as their headless mother, Dean-o?

Shit.

He should have thought of this. New sweat surfaced in a sheen across his body. He was back to the same old agenda, the Find Food and Water routine, but now it was doubly important. He had babies to feed. Thousands of tiny new bellies to fill, along with his now empty gut.

I can't just sit here. The clock is ticking. I've got to get moving. And NOW!

With that thought, quick and urgent as it came, the suit abandoned the remains of its pudding and began to crawl west, towards the heartland. Dean couldn't help but acknowledge this second instance of collusion between his desires and the actions of the roaches surrounding him.

And while this fact made him strangely proud, something at the back of his mind recoiled. Because communication was a two way road, and roaches must certainly have desires of their own.

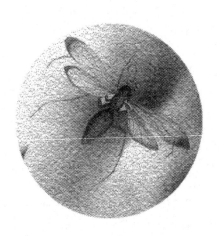

Chapter Five

Time played tricks. Could be decompressing. Could be redacting. Dean had no watch, and day and night were old memories. Kid stuff. The new grown up reality was this: darkness/food/water/fire. Stay moving.

Primal shit.

Days passed. At least, what *felt* like days. Dean tried to calculate mileage, to figure a way to gauge time by distance traveled. It was a waste. His internal atlas was nonexistent. His last score on a geography test- Mrs. Beeman's class, 5th grade- was a D minus.

Even if the road signs weren't blazed or shattered, Dean would barely have known where he was. Sense of place wasn't part of his make-up. But he felt that the best plan was to keep moving inland. Pick a major road and stick with it. Keep walking.

The upside being that sleep didn't halt his progress. When he was on the ground- snoring, twitching through his

REM state- the bugs kept moving. They were relentless in their drive.

Dean was awakened once, by the sensation of his crash helmet sliding against a surface with more yield than the roadway he was used to being dragged along while resting. The roaches had veered off into a field- they'd hit farm territory just hours before- and found the crispy remains of what might have been a baby goat. Dean managed to tear off a chunk of it and sequester it to the wide top of his left boot. He'd need to wash it off before he could eat it. Couldn't just dive in like his insectile friends. If he got desperate he guessed he could just peel away most of the outside of the meat and maw down its center. Maybe the fallout didn't get in that deep.

The temperature seemed to have leveled out around a chilly forty-or-so degrees. It pulled the moisture from Dean's face and hands and left his skin feeling tight and chapped. He guessed his face was stuck in a sort of permanent grimace. A charming look, he was certain.

Thirst was always nagging him. He made do with the occasional thin puddle of water that either hadn't been vaporized or had resettled, and once he found a decent batch, maybe a gallon, still tucked inside a fractured chunk of irrigation pipe. With nothing to contain it in he was forced to gulp down what he could and make sure the roaches took the rest.

I could always eat some of the bugs if I got too hungry. I'm sure there's some water in their bodies, and they'd understand. They'd be eating each other right now if my sewing job didn't have them all in assigned seating.

But the thought felt wrong. Mutinous. They were working together now, or at least it seemed like it. He'd stopped short of giving them each names, but he felt an at-

tachment to the bugs. They understood him. They shared his
motto: Do Not Die.

No. They'd survive this together.

But why?

Dean was giving up whatever marginal hope he'd had
of finding either a rich food source, other living beings, or
both. When he traveled through cities, or whatever was left
of them, he was able to acquire a few things. A sturdy hiking
backpack from the remaining third of a ravaged outdoor store.
A thick plastic bottle for water. Remnants of cloth and thin
tinder wood (usually partially burnt) to make torches for light-
ing the way as the un-natural winter worsened. He'd edged
around a still-flaming gas-tank crater and found a small fridge
with three diet sodas inside. It was hideous shit but Dean
knew he couldn't afford to be picky right now. He used one
of the diet sodas to clean the radiation from his stashed chunk
of toasty goat meat. If the cola could remove the rust from
airplane parts, it ought to be able to deal with a little nuclear
waste.

It was *not* fine dining, nowhere near pudding-good,
but Dean wolfed it down and kept moving. He couldn't wear
the backpack for fear of disturbing his suit, so he tied it to his
waist with a length of twine and let it drag behind him, whether
walking on foot or traveling by roach. The pack was pretty
sturdy and helped him keep his motley assortment of goods in
one place. And if it started to fall apart Dean figured he could
use the sewing skills he'd learned constructing his outfit to fix
it.

Finally- at the borders of a suburb Dean had named
Humvington for its sheer numbers of blazed-out SUV frames-
he made a valuable find. There, inside a half-melted tackle-
box, Dean found a pair of thick gloves with leather across the

palms and the finger tips cut off. It was a blessing, and for a few hours Dean felt a renewed sense of vigor. He was semi-equipped, alive, and heading places.

But the further he went the more he realized his efforts might be pointless no matter which direction he hiked. As insane as it seemed, no one else was alive.

The global imaging satellites and tiny computer chips guiding the missiles that hit America had done a *flawless* job. Every time Dean reached some new urban center he was confronted by fresh blast craters. Instead of clearing the radioactivity he'd tried to leave behind, he was charging into new ellipses of damage, places that would take much more than weeks to be livable again. And whenever Dean dared venture into buildings or homes in search of life he was greeted by the same thing:

Death. Unrestrained and absolute.

Exposed finger-bones pointing accusations at the sky.

Baby replicas composed of ash, mouths still open in a cry.

The bodies of a man and his dog fused together, skin and fur melded. Nobody wanted to die alone.

WWIII was less a war than it was a singular event. A final reckoning for a race sick of waiting for the next pandemic to clean things up. And since Dean never saw any sign of invasion, or even recon, he guessed that most of the other countries were now sitting in the same smoking squalor.

Each new region was the same. Crucial buildings, city centers, food stores- all dusted. He had much better chances of productive forage at the outskirts of cities, and then it was back into the blackness and the road to the next noxious burg.

It was during this seemingly timeless stretch of travel

that Dean started to find *them*. The other ones like Dean.

He understood the zeitgeist, and how the media had allowed the entire planet to experience the same set of stimuli. So Dean shouldn't have been so surprised that others would have tried to protect themselves like he had.

But their ideas- their suits- were so bad. Crackpot, really. At least Dean's knowledge of entomology, passed down from his Ivy League father, had given him some viable theory to work on. And he had to assume that the President's Twinkie suit was based on top-level Pentagon science that didn't quite hit the right calculations. But these poor folks, they'd just been guessing.

Styrofoam man had surrounded himself with customized chunks of beverage coolers. Most of the enterprise had melted right into the guy's skin. Hadn't he ever tried to cook some sweet-and-sour soup leftovers in the microwave?

The cinder block guy had a better idea, but it appeared that the pneumatics that were supposed to give him mobility had burned out in the first wave of fire. Dean had crawled up on the suit to check and confirmed that the man had died of heat exposure and dehydration. Without being able to move he'd spent his last days trapped inside a concrete wall, right there in the middle of the street.

The lady Dean found who was wearing two leather aprons and steel-toed work boots on each of her four appendages? He couldn't even force that to make a lick of sense. But she appeared to have died from exposure. She was missing great swaths of her hair and was face down in a pool of black and red that was probably a portion of her lungs.

This was the response of the populace. Madness in the face of madness.

Dean found one man who was actually breathing, although it didn't look like that'd be going on much longer. His body was laid out in a splayed X in the yard of a smoldering duplex, next to the melted pink remains of a lawn flamingo coated in grey ash. The man's eyes had gone milky white with cataracts and the smell on the body was bad meat incarnate. But the chest was rising and falling ever so faintly.

Could be my eyes fooling me. A flashback from that bad pudding.

Dean squatted in closer to the man's body and noticed how loose and wrinkled his face was. He'd never seen skin so rumpled, like one of those fancy dogs they put in motivational posters at work.

Dean gently pressed the middle and forefinger of his left hand against the man's neck to check for a pulse.

It was this motion that caused the man's face to slide off of his head.

Not only that, the man changed colors. His first wrinkled face was stark white. His new face was light brown. The same cataract-coated eyes peered out at the heavy sky.

As if from the shock of losing his first face, he stopped breathing.

God damn it! I finally find someone and now they're gone.

Dean couldn't take it. Everyone he'd met since the bomb dropped was either dead or potentially imaginary.

Maybe it's not too late.

Unsure of what exactly he was doing, Dean attempted to perform CPR. But his hands kept slipping from side to side and it was hard to center over the man's chest. This man's surface was so *loose*....

He must be wearing someone else's entire skin!

Dean ripped open the man's shirt. Dean freaked. Stitches up the center of the abdomen and chest. Industrial floss or fishing line, Dean couldn't tell. Skin dry and puckered at the puncture points. Horror-show shit.

Dean tugged at the sutures/got a finger hold/got them to slip loose. He laid back dead white skin and uncovered brown slicked with blood and Vaseline. Tried to swipe the goop off the guy's chest. Succeeded. Started compressions without the slippage.

Dean wished he had paddles. Wished he could just yell "Clear" and shock this guy back into the world of the living.

The compressions weren't doing much. Dean moved north and started blowing breath into the man's mouth, fighting back the nausea induced by the smell of lung corruption.

A hand at Dean's forehead, pushing up and away. A moan. He was trying to speak.

"…the fuck are you doing, man? Get up off me!"

"What? Okay, just stay calm."

"Tell me to stay calm. I'm just lying here in my yard and you think you can molest my ass. That's fucked up, man. Fucked up. For real."

"I wasn't molesting you. You had stopped breathing. I was doing CPR."

"Seriously?"

"Yeah."

"Well, alright then. I've been confused. Didn't mean to snap at you, man. I'm not feeling right. Haven't been for a couple of days. Name's Wendell."

Wendell strained to raise his left hand, still coated in dead pale skin. Dean took the hand, felt slippage.

"I'm Dean. Wendell, I think you might be very sick."

"No shit, genius. You a doctor? Part of a rescue team?"

"No. I'm just a guy."

"Just a guy, huh? Maybe you can tell me what's going on. I mean, I know the bombs dropped, I was ready for that, with my mojo and all… but do you know if the whole U.S. got hit? Is there someplace we could get to better than this joint?"

"I don't know much, Wendell. I know I've been traveling for a couple of days and haven't seen anything but destruction. I was starting to lose hope, but now I've found you and I guess that's a good sign. Maybe there are more people like us who survived the first wave."

"What about…hey… what about… do you know if they got our president? Is there somebody out there with rescue plans, working on rebuilding."

Dean realized the real answer to this question might just shock Wendell right back into the grave so he opted for a simple out.

"The president's gone. There are no plans that I know of."

"Wish you had better news, but I can't say I'm going to miss that stupid cracker motherfucker. Hell, I figure he's a big part of why I'm laid out here right now."

"Yeah…hey, you called him a 'cracker.' Do you hate white people? Did you think the 'white devil' would live through the bombing? Is that why you're wearing this guy's skin?"

"What skin? You mean my Mojo? Oh, no, that's got nothin' to do with color. I've had plenty of white friends and now they're just as dead as anybody. No, my Mojo is all about good luck. See, my friend Peter, he lives…pardon, used to live… three blocks down from my house and I swear he was the luckiest motherfucker I ever met. Never saw a lotto ticket he didn't recoup on. Lucked into not one but *two* boats at the expo raffle last year. The odds were always in his favor."

"So you skinned him?"

"Patience, man. Don't jump ahead. You got somewhere to be?"

"Not really, I guess."

"What about food or drink? You got somethin' for me? Might as well ask since you busted in and interrupted the flow of my story."

"I've got a couple of packets of fruit snacks and two diet sodas."

"Diet soda? Goddamn! That gunk is terrible for you. Full of aspartame. You know the guys that work with that stuff have to wear biohazard suits?"

"I hadn't heard that, Wendell. Do you want one? It's all I've got."

"Normally I wouldn't, but I'm pretty parched. I'd probably still take you up on it if all you had to offer was a bucket of cat piss."

Dean cracked a can. That pop and hiss of released carbonation was comforting somehow. Familiar. An old sound from what now felt like a whole different age.

He handed the can to Wendell.

"Thanks, man." As Wendell was bringing it towards his lips, the soda slipped from his hand and hit the ground rolling. Dean snagged it and tipped it back upright, trying to save whatever he could.

"See, Dean, my goddamn Mojo ain't worth a barbecued shit. It's too lose. I thought Peter and I were about the same size, but I guess he wore slimming clothes. Maybe his good luck always made him look skinnier than he really was. Who knows?"

Dean helped Wendell tip the soda can to his lips. He took a deep slug and winced.

"Hurts going down. Can't be good."

Dean didn't offer any solace. He was amazed this guy was talking at all.

"Okay, back to my story. The deal is, Peter's got more luck than sense. And his one big mistake, I guess, was thinking he'd be lucky enough to get away with fucking my wife, Gladys. But maybe something in his good fortune shifted. I don't know. And this is about a week and a half back, when the news got all crazy and the President disappeared and nobody would answer any questions for nobody about what was going on. You remember that feeling in the air? Like we were all dead for sure? Like it was just a matter of time?"

Dean nodded.

"Well, I think that feeling made some people do the things they always wanted to. So Peter, who'd always had an eye for my wife- I mean, I'd seen him looking at her at church no less- he decided it was his time to take a poke at her. And I caught 'em, right in the middle of their rutting, under the laundry line in the back yard. They were biting each other, and…um… smacking each other. Pulling hair and shit. You could tell this was something they'd wanted in about forever. I had a little flip-out gator knife on my belt. And, uh, I guess I jumped right into the same pile of crazy they'd been rolling around in. The rest I'm sure you can figure."

Another nod from Dean.

"But the thing I should have thought of was that things had *changed*. We'd entered our end-times. The rules were different. They had to be. Otherwise Peter's lucky streak would have continued and I never would have known any better. So I should have figured that all that good luck was gone, and never tried to wear it over me. I wished this thing…" Wendell pinched at the dead face that lay next to him, a thick fold of it in his fingers, "would protect me, but it didn't. It wasn't really the Mojo I'd hoped for. It was just some dead asshole's skin. And now… now I'm dyin' in it."

There were tears in Wendell's cloudy blind eyes. Dean wanted to give him a hug, but the roaches hadn't eaten in a while, and the last time he'd wrapped his arms around someone they'd been eaten whole. Call it a non-option.

The best Dean could do was take off his gloves and hold the man's hand. But not for long. This man would die soon, and Dean didn't want to be around for that.

So, as Wendell's breath slowed and he seemed to float into some layer of sleep, Dean released the man's hand. Then he let the roaches hit the ground and begin their steady westward crawl, leaving all forms of bad mojo behind them.

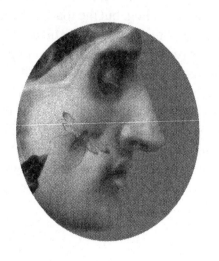

Chapter Six

Three more days- maybe four- passed. Dean and his suit made good time. In another, less nuclear world this whole ambulatory clothing thing might have sold great to people who wanted to conserve fuel. The ASPCA and PETA would have complained, sure. That was what they did. But the rest of the world didn't give a damn about insects. Get them past their initial revulsion, make it look pretty and clean, and you've got a best-seller.

During his travel Dean acquired two loaves of rye bread, one jar pureed vegetable baby food, one scarf with the words "Winter Fun" embroidered on it, three gallons unfiltered water in various containers, and one overall sense of crushing ennui.

To keep busy and clear his mind he handled a lot of the footwork himself and periodically checked his suit for birthsigns. So far the host of egg cases adorning him remained in gestation, but they looked darker. Soon the nymphs would be here, demanding sustenance.

He kept the "Winter Fun" scarf wrapped- very lightly- around his face and crossed his fingers. He had to keep breathing but guessed that the air quality around him would petrify even coal miners.

So far, though, there were no signs of the cellular corruption that had taken Boot Lady and Wendell to their graves.

A day ago he'd woken from his sleep to the sound of flowing water. He'd popped up quickly enough to run down to the river's edge and fill the containers he'd amassed in his backpack.

Could have been the Ohio River. Could have been the Mississippi. He cursed his D minus geography skills and wished he knew. But since then he'd been heading south, probably a few hundred yards from the river at any time. It seemed crazy to abandon a water source, but it also seemed crazy to stay still when they were certainly in a dead zone. Besides, if he made it to the gulf perhaps he could find a boat and head south to a less ravaged continent. Who would bomb Peru? Somebody who hated llamas?

The clouds overhead remained black as ever, but also seemed to emit a low luminescence that coated Dean's path like filthy moonlight. Maybe his sight was just adjusting.

Any longer in the dark like this and I'll be pure white with pink eyes, finding my way with echolocation. Interplanetary spelunkers will find me and call me a wondrously adaptive creature. Look at how he works in concert with the roaches that surround him!

That was the other thing bothering Dean. When he wasn't fighting off a sense of weary resignation and trying to chase away the self-destructive worries that paralyzed him, he found himself experimenting with the seemingly stronger link between his desires and the actions of the suit.

He could make patches of the outfit skitter faster than others. He executed circles and vertical rolls. He could choose which group of clustered mouths would drink from his carefully poured puddles of water. Most disturbing, he found that if he concentrated hard enough he could get them to twirl their feelers in clockwise or counter-clockwise directions. The sensation that ran through his mind when this occurred wasn't anything he recognized. It was a thin, high-pitched buzzing and he could swear he felt it in his bones and at the spot where skull and spine met. It made his skin itch a bit, but it wasn't totally unpleasant. In fact, the sensation was seductively mind-clearing. No more doubt. No more concerns over the *meaning* of being alive.

It was the *feeling* of being alive, and nothing else. Existence without thought.

Dean tried not to engage in this sort of thing too often, but there was little else to do, especially when he took feeding breaks. No TV's to watch. No magazines to flip through while noshing down veggie mush on rye.

It was after one of these enchanting culinary pit stops that Dean noticed the tiny moving lights in the distance.

They were slight at best, damn near microscopic from this far away, moving across his path in the direction of the river. Each of them was uniform distance from the other and moving at a quick pace.

Dean closed the distance, slowed slightly by the water-heavy bag he was towing.

The closer he got, the more familiar the motions of the lights seemed. Like something from one of Daddy Dean

Sr.'s bug documentaries. They had to be glowing insects of some sort. No other animals moved that low or that orderly.

When Dean was within inches of the line of shuffling light he crouched down and removed his goggles to try and see more clearly.

What the hell is this?

As hard as Dean focused his eyes, all he could see were tiny sections of leaves, each with a faint sort of phosphorescence.

Then he felt the buzzing at the tip of his spine. He honed in on it, cultivated the sensation until he picked up its tone.

Fear. He could feel the roaches' legs twitching a hundred yard dash through the cold, damp air.

A glow to his left. Before he could turn his head- a voice. Female.

"Don't move. The bugs are panicked because you are surrounded. There are thousands of soldiers on every side you."

"Soldiers? Where?"

"Look down."

Dean tilted his head towards the ground. There, aided by the glow coming from the woman, he could see them. Ants. Big ones, thick enough to make a popping noise if stepped upon. An armada of them, crawling over each other, maintaining a tight circle around the space he was crouched in.

"If you reach out to touch the foragers you will be swarmed by soldiers. This is what they do. This is *all* they do. I can try to stop them but their instinct will likely rule out whatever control I have."

Dean believed her. There was an earnest and concerned tone to her voice that reminded him of the time his father warned him not to get too close to his prize bombardier beetle. *He'll blind you without a thought, Dean.* That's what his father had said.

"So what do I do now?"

"Stand up. Slowly. Then take a few very wide steps back from the foragers' trail. They'll no longer perceive you as a threat."

Dean did as he was told. His knees felt loose and shaky with each step he took, but soon he was ten feet from the steadily marching troop of leaf-bearing ants and their protectors.

"Good. That was good. You got too close."

She sounded exasperated. How much danger had he been in? What the hell was going on?

Dean turned to face the woman.

Holy shit...now the ants are swarming her...they're everywhere...

"What can I do? How should I help you?"

Dean ran over to his back pack and fumbled for the zipper.

I'll get my water and douse her with it. I'll wash those little fuckers away.

"What are you doing?" she asked. Her voice was now perfectly calm. Post-sex mellow. Almost amused.

"I can get them off of you. Hold on just a second..." his hands were shaking but he had a grip on the zipper now. "I've got something that can save you."

He felt her glow coming towards him. Caught graceful strides from his periphery.

"My dear man, I'm not looking for a savior." The voice was confident, with a hint of laughter behind it.

Dean let go of the zipper and looked up at her. She

had a thin hand outstretched in his direction. It was free of ants but had a coat of... something... over it. The rest of her was covered in ants of various shapes and sizes, hundreds of thousands of them shuttling around, touching each others antennae, carrying bits of shining wet plant matter.

She was, aside from the ants, entirely nude.

"I'm Mave," she said. "Now you. Who exactly the hell are you? And where did you get that fabulous suit?"

Chapter Seven

She had a place of her own, a tattered tarp lean-to backed by a portion of white picket fence. Where she rested, it used to be the backyard garden of some family that no longer existed. She said she'd always wanted a white picket fence. Corny, but true.

Dean had shaken off his initial shock and introduced himself back at the roadway. He'd told her a very abridged version of his own story-omitting the appearance of Yahmuhwesu, who he still believed might have been a hallucination- as they walked back to her current digs. She had questions along the way.

"Twinkies?" and

"Goat marinated in diet soda! That tasted hideous, right?" and

"The guy really thought Styrofoam would work?" and

"Did you check Wendell to see if he wasn't wearing a couple more layers of skin? Maybe there was a Mexican or

Asian guy deeper down?" and

"Do you know how close you just came to being killed?"

And she smiled every time she questioned him.

How can she be so happy at a time like this? Isn't she afraid the ants will get inside her mouth.

Dean knew she wasn't. Whatever rudimentary mental link he'd founded between himself and the roaches, she blew that out of the water. The ants- she called them Acromyrmex or leafcutters as if the names were interchangeable- never crossed her lips. They never scuttled into her eyes. They did crawl through her shoulder length black hair, but didn't mat it with the bright fungus they were growing on her skin. And although he tried not to look, they didn't appear to hover around the folds of her vagina.

She walked carefully and avoided resting her limbs against her body. Didn't want to crush any of the Acromyrmex. Couldn't stand the lemony smell they made when they died.

Here, at her new garden, the ground burst upward with miniature rolling hills.

"The rest of the colony. They can produce a certain amount of fungus on my skin- my perspiration actually seems to speed its growth, which was unexpected- but it really requires a more total darkness to produce the gongylidia. That's the key part of their harvest. The stuff they feed to the babies."

At the mention of the word "babies" Dean felt a sudden need to inspect his suit.   So far, so stagnant. The tiny eggs remained whole. Thank goodness.

"Oh, that's right." Mave smiled, watching him. "You're the pregnant one! Yahmuhwesu told me about you."

"Pardon me?"

"Yahmuhwesu. The collective unconsciousness guy. Fiery chariot and all that… Oh, come on. Don't make that face. I know you know exactly who I'm talking about. He met you before he appeared in front of Terry and me. But when he spoke with us he figured you'd die before you ever had a chance to give birth."

Dean tasted vomit and goat in his mouth. This was too much all at once. His shock must have shown on his face because Mave had furrowed her brow.

"Shit. It's a bitch to take in this sort of info, isn't it? And here I am just dumping it all over you… sorry. Listen, when he met you he taught you how to do that humming trick, right? The tonal language. If you can lock into my tone I think we might be able to communicate better. Something about the nature of speaking like that that cuts out a lot of the filters."

She didn't wait for him to respond. She simply straightened her spine, closed her eyes, and started humming.

The sound was lullaby-beautiful. Dean couldn't help but move closer to it.

He started to hum in return, closing his eyes and listening as hard as he could, trying to find the exact range in which she was vibrating.

He hit it. They locked in. Their eyes popped open. He took in grey pupils with flecks of gold in them. Her eyes were gorgeous. He couldn't look away.

Is she even human?

"Of course I'm human."

"Oh, yeah. You're in my thoughts now." He blushed, heat blooming across his face.

"And you're in my thoughts, too. And since we don't have too much time, we need to start figuring things out."

"Wait. Why don't we have time?"

"I'll get to that. Soon. But for now I just need to know that we're thinking in line with each other so we can make the right plan."

Thunder cracked in the dust-heap clouds above.

"Mave, have you noticed that this process seems to stir up the clouds?"

"Uh-huh. I wonder if lightning will strike us if we stay like this for too long... Doesn't matter. Stay with me here. I've got a couple of things to tell you.

"First- Yahmuhwesu is real, or at least, he's as real as anything else on this planet. He- at least I think it's a he- visited you. He visited Terry and me. And I'd imagine that if anyone else managed to live through this ridiculous nuclear fuck-up, Yahmuhwesu's visited them too. And I think, as far as gods go, that Yahmuhwesu is a bit on the crazy side. Or at least, he's *confused*. So he's playing with us. I'm sure you've noticed some changes in yourself recently."

"Yeah, I have. The roaches have been listening to me. To my thoughts. Doing what I want. And I think I'm listening to them a smidgen too. There's this buzzing sound at the back of my head that I used to create by thinking at them, trying to communicate. But now it's just... there. It's very quiet. And it makes me itch."

"And, Dean, you're not dead. *You're not dead.* Didn't you wonder why Wendell's lungs had ruptured but you're able to traipse around drinking atomic water and sleeping in ash? I think you, and me, and Terry, we'd all be goners right now if we hadn't been visited. Sure, that suit may have helped you survive the blast by some ridiculous miracle, but it can't be *only* that."

"You think Yahmuhwesu did something to us?"

"Look at me, Dean. I wasn't born the world's biggest walking anthill. This is something fresh, something I woke to just as Yahmuhwesu disappeared. He definitely made this happen. You may have grown up with comic books, Dean, but in real life you've got to know that gamma rays toast people. They vomit until they taste their guts. It's terrible. So if the nuclear explosion didn't do this, I can guarantee our vanishing deity did. There are no other feasible answers. It's an Occam's Razor scenario... Do you know what I used to do, Dean?"

"Ballet?" It wasn't an intentional compliment. Dean had never been that smooth. But he had noticed how strong and sleek her legs looked. Spring-loaded.

"No, not ballet. I was never that coordinated. I was an entomologist, just like your father. Just like Terry. And I'd devoted my life to these ants. Acromyrmex. The leafcutters. They're truly beautiful creatures, easily the pinnacle of social and technological expression in ants. That's what I said in my papers when I was working out of U of M. Cultivated my own nest mounds using a queen and fungi shipped up from the Guanacaste province of Coast Rica.

"I watched that queen every day and saw how hard she worked to grow a culture. Tending to the fungus and her eggs. Aerating soil. Creating a whole new world on her own. It was the most incredible thing I'd ever seen, and I felt something then, something far beyond myself. It faded, but when I saw Yahmuhwesu appear it came back again, and fierce. And whatever that feeling was, he filled me up with it, to the brim. Everything seemed clearer, the interconnectedness of all life, matter, energy, everything. He told me I had a new purpose here, among my 'subjects.' That was the word he used. And when I woke up from whatever fugue I was in, I had become the new queen.

"I could feel them in my brain. Calling to me. Like that buzz you describe. Only it didn't make me itch. It made me... wet. I could feel waves rolling through my belly. I got gooseflesh. My breath ran short. Panting. I buckled twice on the way to the lab and the nest. Because I could hear them. They were still alive. The university's lab was underground and somehow intact. And they needed me. I didn't even think of how I'd abandoned Terry back at the shelter."

"Wait, who is this Terry guy? You were with him when Yahmuhwesu appeared to you?"

"Yeah, but I need to finish telling you about these ants. I think it's important, somehow, that you understand them. Because they are part of me now. They have been ever since I managed to crawl my way through the rubble and get access to the nest mound."

She related the rest of it then, how she'd dug down through the soil and found the existing mother queen and swallowed her whole. How the future mother queens-fledgling tribe-bearers who were meant to eventually carry eggs and fungal spores outward to start new nests- had all crawled to her then, running up her legs, crawling inside of her and resting against the walls of her uterus, triggering orgasms that left her shaking for hours. And after that the rest of the tribe had filed out- tiny food workers/minimas/foragers/soldiers- each finding their place on her body and immediately starting to do their jobs however they could.

"I'm still me. Still Mave," she said, "but now I'm also this colony. My mind contains their hive mind.

"What I don't understand, yet, is what this new fungus is, or why it glows, or why it grows so goddamned fast. Even a hint of it on the jaw of a forager will instantly attach itself to a cutting. That's why the fragments you saw crossing the road were already bright.

"This fungus didn't originate with any of the queens inside; they came to me with nothing other than their instinct. So... I think the new fungus is coming from *me*. But I don't know how, so I've been holed up here to try and study it. Some of the ponds and riverbanks near here have vital plant life right at the edge of the water. We need it to really make the colony grow."

"We?"

"Yes, I told you that I'm their queen. I guess I'm using the royal we. And we're the ones who need your help."

He looked at her then, this strange new woman and her legion of tiny ants and her grey/gold eyes. The leafcutters were everywhere on her now, most holding little glowing slivers of plant matter that swayed in the winds and gave her an appearance of profound life, of a majesty that made him want to serve her despite the buzz at the base of his head that was screaming "Run- we can survive best alone."

"What am I supposed to do?"

"That what I'm not quite sure of. I know that we can't stay here much longer, though I'd like to."

"Picket fence?"

"Yeah. That and the nest. But the plant life here was scarce to begin with, and we've already processed most of what remains in the area. Plus, I think Terry might find us."

"Why is that bad?"

"Terry was an entomologist too, before the bombs hit and made everyone's job titles obsolete. That's how I knew him. We both worked out of the university. We were lovers in a purely pragmatic way. We understood the need. The pheromones.

"He was renting an old house in the suburbs south of campus. It was Cold War equipped- bomb shelter in the back yard. We screwed down there for kicks. He wore a gas mask. We passed out holding each other in an army cot and didn't wake up until we felt the concussion of the first bomb exploding. Total dumb luck that we lived.

"Then, when we crawled out a few days later, there was a glowing god waiting for us. Terry could barely handle the shock of all of it. He was crying one second, furious the next. Unstable. Then Yahmuhwesu hummed his way into our heads and changed us. I haven't seen Terry since.

"That's why I'm afraid. Because if Yahmuhwesu affected Terry the same way he did with us, then right now Terry is hunting down a hive of his own."

"More leafcutters?"

"I wish. Terry's bug of choice was the *Nomamyrmex*, Dean. Army ants."

"That's bad?"

"It's terrible. If he manages to find a hive in nature there will be millions of them. And if his mind is as fragile as I believe it to be then Terry will become an instrument of the hive instead of the other way around."

"You don't think he could control them?"

"I don't think he'd even try. He was always so clinical. His brain wasn't equipped for this sort of metaphysical shift. I grew up with hippies in a commune and started meditating with my imaginary friends when I was four years old. I've always desired a more mystical reality, despite my chosen field of work.

"And you, your single-minded drive to stay alive appears to usurp any need for reality.

"But Terry, his brain probably split in two the moment

that first bomb dropped and he realized he wasn't ever going to have a cup of Starbucks coffee again."

Dean wanted to laugh, for a moment, but he saw how serious the look in Mave's eyes was. This was dire. The leafcutter ants that covered her were frantic, almost disorganized in their movements.

"Dean, if Terry does unearth a Nomamyrmex colony they'll be *starving*."

"So they'll eat Terry?"

"If we're lucky. But, assuming he's still conscious by then, they'll know what he knows. That there is a veritable smorgasbord waiting for them in the basement of the U of M lab. And when they don't find them there they'll be able to follow our scent trail."

"They eat leafcutters?"

"For centuries the Acromyrmex has been the favorite food of the army ant. Particularly the queens. They'll sacrifice thousands of their fighters in battle to get a good chance at a fat, juicy mother ant. They'll drag her, still living, all the way back to their tunnels, and then slowly pull the eggs from her body and eat them until she collapses and dies. She is consumed last. A victory feast."

Dean saw Mave recoil at this, felt a scared tremor enter the cross-tuned vibrations relaying thought between the two of them.

"Dean, I *am* the Acromyrmex now. I and the colony might be all that is left of us on Earth. And if we can't find a way to move from this place soon, we'll be eaten alive."

Chapter Eight

The long stretch of internal communication had wiped them out but left them wary. Exhausted, they shuffled over to the fence and agreed to sleep in shifts before figuring out how they could travel.

Dean lay near Mave in the lean-to for a few hours, watching the sleepless march of the ants as they moved over her and traveled back and forth to their garden nest. She had been right about the beauty of the creatures. While Dean admired the tenacity and strength of the cockroach, they lacked the grace and civility and immense complexity that made observing the leafcutter such a pleasure.

The roaches knew how to stay alive, but for what? He tried to cut the question off in his mind, knowing the sense of existential dread that was sure to follow any attempted answer.

Dean's father had built up a life for himself. He had done much more than simply "get by." An esteemed figure in his field. Research papers published in all the right magazines. A loving son who helped him through his years as a young widower. But in the end a ridiculous auto accident took his life. His papers and ideas were replaced by newer ones that failed to credit him. His son flipped out and traveled the world squandering the money the father had saved up for years. No, Daddy Dean Sr. had existed for nothing. And now the last of his bloodline was surrounded by semi-empathic roaches and trapped in a wasteland, lying next to a fungus-coated woman with exotic ants in her womb.

Actually, Dean thought, his dad might have been really intrigued by that last part, but it wasn't what you necessarily hoped for when you had a kid.

After a while Mave opened her eyes (those *eyes*) and within seconds Dean allowed himself to drift into a shallow sleep.

He dreamed- army ants marching/his face consumed by baby roaches/Terry chewing his way through Mave's vagina. He woke screaming. Mave placed her hand on his forehead, the smell of her fungus rich and almost sweet near his nose. He calmed. He caught another hour of shut eye. This time real slumber.

But at waking the dreams still chilled him. They lingered. From the look in *her* eyes, she'd somehow shared his fear.

They hit the road within hours.

Travel time moved on the following agenda:

Head back north, then west when the river branches. Stay close to the water. More likely to find some sort of plant life there. Get far enough west and Mave knew of a place where there might be safety. A military liaison to the university had once been sweet on her and spilled post-coital secrets to impress, including the general location of a military stronghold they'd built out of a natural cave system. The place was supposed to have some degree of sustainability. Which meant flowing water and clean air. Which could mean weapons with which a person or persons could effectively stave off an invasion of army ants. Which *might* mean a self-contained bio-system that she and Dean could adapt their insectile selves to.

Travel time was a bitch.

They tried to drag part of the Acromyrmex nest behind them on top of her old lean-to tarp. That meant slowgoing. That meant frenzied waste workers cleaning out dead ants/collapsed tunnels/reduced gongylidia output. That meant confused foragers hunting dead land for any plant life at all, coming back with empty, ashy mandibles. The fungus across Mave's skin began to lose its luster without new plant life to culture on. The crumbs and trash they tried to adhere to her made her look diseased.

The new queen was upset. Dean would hear her humming, but not in a frequency he could even try to reach. He guessed she was calming the colony; asking them to endure. He knew the sound of her excited his roaches. Their cerci swayed to the sound.

He watched Mave's movements, the sway of her hips, the way her feet seemed to keep moving without real exertion.

For some reason her beauty pitched him double lonely. She would never have a guy like Dean, would she? He considered running ahead, leaving the queen and her dying colony and heading west to the Pacific by himself. She'd only slow him down, maybe even bring a horde of ravenous ants with huge jaws his way.

He could be free. A lone wolf. He'd finally tattoo his knuckles with his motto, four letters across each fist:

DONOTDIE

But was that all he really felt now? He wasn't sure. Those grey/gold eyes kept him unstable.

Maybe we could spend the rest of our time together. Maybe we can find some place with a white picket fence and forty acres out back for nesting.

So for now Dean kept things left foot/right foot/re-peat and followed the queen of the dying leafcutters along the river.

Chapter Nine

"It's getting warmer, don't you think? Brighter, too."

Mave had demanded they sit by the river for a while to let her ants search for some plant life and harvest proteins from their collapsing nest.

Dean thought she was right about the warmth. He hadn't worn his "Winter Fun" scarf for the last fifteen miles or so. He'd guessed he was heating up from exertion- dragging a backpack full of water and a tarp full of dirt was a gut-buster- but maybe Mave was on point.

He hoped she *wasn't* correct for a few reasons:

1. Dean was sure the cold was all that'd kept the now fantastic number of eggs on his suit from hatching. Currently he and Mave were located nowhere near a worthy stash of baby roach food.

2. The Nuclear Summer theory- Following nuclear winter the ozone layer and stratosphere are effectively destroyed. UV light would torch any

remaining territory that wasn't already turned to desert by the lack of photosynthesis during the blackout. Anything that had a harsh time with UV light before would really feel the burn. Genetic defects galore. Polar ice caps would melt. Continental flooding. The greenhouse effect in fast fast forward. Even sea life would go stagnant, except for those weird things that live off of gas vents at the bottom of the Marianas Trench.
3. As much as he would welcome a bit of light, it freaked his suit out and ravaged the leafcutter's fungus. They'd both be in even more of a pinch with the sun blazing overhead.

However, he was enjoying the increased sensation of warmth in the air, slight though it was. He laid back against the gentle slope of the riverbank and watched the cancerous clouds churn overhead. He thought, even at this distance from her, that he could smell Mave's fungus. It calmed him. He relaxed his neck, allowing his crash helmet to sink its heft into the ground. His shoulders dropped.

The sound of the river water running seaward formed a constant white noise soundtrack. He let himself float with it, pictured himself as a drop of water, incapable of death, unknowing, yet immensely important and powerful.

He closed his eyes and let his head tip over in Mave's direction.

The smell of her was sort of like lavender mixed with fresh coffee. It invigorated as much as it soothed. Were there spores of it, he wondered, working their way into his brain right now? He hoped so.

She was sovereign. Let him join her subjects, enthralled.

Two sensations:

Movement without control.

The scent of lemons and hot metal. The smell of ruptured ants.

Dean opened his eyes, instantly awake. He was no longer on the riverbank. The roaches were moving at full-out speed, autonomous of his control, heading towards a nearby copse of charred tree stumps.

A scream in the distance, explosive, and then suddenly cut off.

Mave.

Dean forced his hands and feet to the ground, churning up hardened earth, leaving tracks. The roaches were not stopping. Whatever they had sensed, they wanted to get as far away as possible.

Go with them, Dean! The roaches got you this far. You can keep living.

You can survive.

Their pace never flagged. Now they were just feet from a low hiding spot.

Another shriek. Crunching sounds that rolled Dean's stomach even at this distance.

You know what's happening, Dean. It's Terry. He's found you. He's found Mave. But he wants to eat her first. A big fat juicy mama ant. Now is your only chance to run!

The suit kept crawling, more cautious now, looking for a way to crest the next hill without being seen by anything down below.

Dean dug his heels in harder but couldn't get traction.

Shit shit shit! Mave's dying. Stop this. Do something.

Dean began to hum. He focused his thoughts on the tight space at the back of his skull and tried to bring the sound as close as he could to the buzz that flourished there.

The roaches began to slow. He let the hum drop to a low drone at the back of his throat. The hive mind buzz locked in.

we are scared we are scared predator scared predator scared distance dark distance quiet scared escape distancehidehidehidehidehideprotecthide

Dean didn't hear actual words, but this was the message he received in a language older than any man had ever created. The language of survival.

It was a sound for animals. It ensured a thriving planet. It was old and powerful and he was sure that a hint of that audible pattern echoed inside of every atom of his body.

But it wasn't anything Dean wanted to listen to anymore.

There was something stronger working through his mind now. A brighter sound at the front of his head. A siren's call.

Her spores really did get into my brain.

Dean tuned into the sound. It felt nearly as ancient as the desire to run, to live at all costs. But this sound had a beauty to it. A nobility.

And as he found the right tone in his throat to harmonize there was only one word at the front of his thoughts:

Fight.

He could smell her and the colony on the poison wind. Sweet

fungus. Acidic death. Adrenaline. Pain.

There was another smell in the air, and whether he was pulling it into his mind via his own nose or the roaches receptors he was unsure.

It was the smell of hunger. Desperation.

Dean charged toward it face first, his own feet pushing him onward, workman's boots rubbing his feet raw.

Go in without hesitation. Strike first and then don't stop until she's safe.

He held in a roar, though it raged at the inside of his chest. He let its energy carry him faster.

There- two hundred yards south. A man stood over Mave. Watching her face twist in agony. Her body was covered in moving black shapes, thick ropes of them, orderly lines of assault tearing away at her face/belly/legs.

Nomamyrmex was on the march.

Dean screamed then, hoping the sound would somehow distract even the bugs which were eating away at Mave.

The man- it had to be Terry- rotated to face the sound. He looked right at Dean. One of his eyes was missing. His nose was also absent, replaced by a jagged black triangle bisected by exposed bone.

Despite these obvious deformities, Dean could tell the man was smiling.

Why would he be smili

The earth fell out from beneath Dean and he felt something long and sharp bore through his right leg before he even realized he wasn't running anymore.

"We're diggers. You cah see that ow. It ohly took us a few hours to displace over six meters of dirt alog this ehtire perimeter. Quite astoudeeg, really."

Terry had approached the pit. The noseless fuck.

"We couldit fide as mady sharp sticks as we'd hoped for, but you do what you cad with what you've got, right? Guess we've lucked out that you hit that particular spike as square as you did. Providess."

Dean said nothing. What good would rage do now? He surveyed his surroundings. Narrow dark rift marked by a million ant trails. A chunk of fractured tree branch jammed through his upper thigh, a few slaughtered roaches hanging from its tip. Wound not bleeding too badly. Must have missed the femoral.

"She told us your name is Dee."

"It's Dean."

"That's what I said. I caht quite make all the sowds I used to. I must admit that we were quite huggry on the trip to fide the Acromyrmex. We had to eat pieces of my face. Other parts too."

At that Terry's remaining eye went wide with fear. Absolute panic.

He emitted a cough, a bark of a low tone. His eye snapped back to empty.

His human brain is still trying to assert itself. Jesus, he's scared. He's so scared, the poor bastard. Those ants are inside of his mind and they've been feeding on him for days.

"Listen, Terry, I know you're in there somewhere. I know you're scared. I know they are hurting you and you're confused and the whole world seems wrong right now, but if you can push to the front of your brain and take control you can stop this. They're just ants."

"Quiet!"

With that Dean noticed the black surge cresting over the lip of the makeshift pit. Thousands- no, hundreds of thousands of them. Thick fingertip-sized ants with bulbous split red-horned heads, each meaty half as big as two whole leafcutters. Their jaw musculature visible from feet away.

Pain is coming, and it will not be brief. If nuclear fallout couldn't kill me how long will it take these ants to end it?

Then he heard the sound. A new tone, from up above. Weak, but coming from Mave.

She's still alive.

He felt, instinctively, that he must try and match her sound.

The first wave of ants was on him. At his earlobes. Sinking their mandibles into the roaches that covered him. Tearing away at his fingertips. Trying to get *into* his fresh wound.

He cleared his throat. He pulled in as much air as he could. Ants bit into his lower lip, sought the meat of his tongue.

From the bottom of his lungs Dean let out his matching tone. It found hers. The sounds merged and became a terrible bellow.

This was a call to war. Dean felt it in his bones.

There was a crackling noise- the sound of thousands of dry distended roach eggs tearing open at once.

Dean's delivery day was here. Within seconds he was the proud father to a seething multitude. The tiny nymphs were too small to be crushed in the huge jaws of the Nomamyrmex, over whom they flowed heedlessly.

They washed up out of the trench, a hungry flood with one target.

Dean stood up, shaking loose hundreds of army ants

from his frame. His right leg held. A thick cast of roach nymphs had formed around it, bearing the weight of his broken limb.

He kept his mind focused on Terry. On Terry's face. Those open holes.

Roaches adored dark wet places like that.

Terry turned to run. The nymphs were already halfway up his legs. He made it one stride before the babies had covered his good eye and were piling in to his blasted orbit.

Terry opened his mouth to scream but the only sound Dean could pick up was the rustle of tiny roaches rubbing against each other on their way down the man's throat.

Dean looked away. He hoped they'd kill him soon. He'd tried to focus the nymphs' movement towards Terry's brain but he wasn't sure how long it would take them to chew through to grey matter.

There was a man inside there somewhere. Confused. Violated. Alone.

Shit.

Dean couldn't take it anymore. His suit helped him crawl up out of the pit and over to Terry's twitching body.

Dean shoved one of his gloves in his own mouth. He bit down. He made a two-fisted grab for the sharpened branch that was rammed through his leg. Twisted left. Twisted right. Wailed through a mouthful of wool and leather. Bit down again. Gripped tight. Pulled up and away. Scoped the point of the stick, dripping his own blood, bits of roach still stuck to it.

And then he swung that spear down into Terry's empty eye socket as hard as he possibly could.

Chapter Ten

This is the way Dean looked at it, much later:

One day you go to bed happy. The next day your dad dies. In a stupid, stupid way.

And maybe you give up on the world. Maybe the world forgets you ever existed and you're okay with that. Because you're alive. Not dead. Not anywhere near that sadness again.

Things are easier alone. Nothing to lose = no loss.

But what if *you* die? Isn't that the biggest loss of them all? You're the only one who will ever truly know you were even alive.

So you protect yourself, with a nod to the esteemed Malcolm X, by any means necessary.

But Malcolm, at the moment he'd said that, probably never guessed one of those means would be covering yourself in nasty, nasty insects.

Probably never even came near being a thought in his

head.

His loss. Because he's dead now. And you, you just keep living, no matter what the world throws at you. Nuclear weapons, crazy presidents, toxic fallout, man-made gods with nothing better to do than alter the genetic code of the remaining humans on Earth.

Fucking army ants.

Oh, and loneliness. Lots of loneliness. You always have to fight that one. But maybe everybody does.

At least that was a problem when you were human.

But that's not exactly the case anymore, is it?

Back up.

Start again.

One day you fall asleep happy. Next to a river under a dark sky. Then you wake up and everything has changed. Including you. You changed so much that for the first time you actually *risk* your life.

For what?

Love? It's as good a word as any. It'll do.

And you've gone so crazy with this feeling, call it love, that you find yourself in an absurd situation, humming and moaning at telepathic bugs and killing brainwashed entomologists.

I know.

It sounds silly.

But it feels important at the time. So important that you nearly die from blood loss lying there in a desolate field next to a corpse filled with baby roaches.

Again, you fall asleep. Or perhaps you pass out from blood loss. But you're happy. Not totally happy, but feeling like now maybe your life was really a *life*. Something more than rote respiration for as sustained a period as possible.

Then you wake up and everything has changed so goddamned much you think you're in heaven.

But you're not dead, and neither is she. The one you love. Sure, her original right arm is missing (eaten by army ants you guess), but it appears that some enterprising leafcutter ants have assembled her a new one out of radiant fungus.

These same enterprising bugs have healed up your sundry cuts and wounds and even staved off the infection in your leg with a Streptomyces bacteria that lives on their skin.

A woman once told you these were the best ants on Earth. You now believe her 100%.

As great as those ants are, you might miss your cockroaches.

"I've set them free," she tells you. "They're up there doing what they're meant to do. Making babies and eating death and putting nutrients back into the soil for when the nuclear summer passes and things can grow again."

It's a lot to absorb at once. Losing your friends like that. Finding out the whole Earth has gone Death Valley for the time being. Trying to figure out how this miraculous woman managed to drag your nearly dead/coma patient ass all the way out west to these secret caves. But you accept it all after a while.

To fill time, to try and adjust, you write down everything you can remember. Part of you feels like these journals could be the last memories of the extinct species you used to consider yourself a part of.

You might explore your new home. Filters. Generators. Tunnels and tunnels and tunnels. You guess one of them might run right to the center of the Earth, but you never find that particular path.

The woman you love, her favorite place is the sustainable eco-sphere. She can even farm there, next to her ants. But they do a pretty great job without her.

All those rooms- the ones that were supposed to house the soldiers and U.S. officials who weren't ready when the bombs hit- they start filling up with the glowing fungal tufts the ants produce. Aside from that it's dark down there, wherever you want it to be.

One day (or night-who can tell down here?) you fall asleep lonely. Then you wake up the next morning and the woman you love is on top of you. She's lifting her hips and putting you inside of her and making every other Best Moment of Your Life seem pretty pale. And when she's done and you're done you hold each other tight and watch as three luminous Acromyrmex queens emerge from between her legs and crawl up to her belly.

Their wings dry. They shiver/shake/touch antennae.

They take flight.

You can tell that they're headed to the surface- nuclear summer bound.

Their movement through the air is heavy with theft.

This makes the woman you love cry. But she is smiling through the tears.

Beaming, really.

For she believes, as you do, that she has just given birth to the first strange children of that terrible new sun.

The Real End of the Line (Maybe)

By Jeremy Robert Johnson

Sometimes when I complete a short story it doesn't feel like it's really finished. Oh, sure, maybe the central conflict is resolved or there was a pretty sentence at the end of the thing that made it feel like that story was done, but something about the character or scenario still sticks with me. Such was the case with my short story "The Sharp Dressed Man at the End of the Line" from *Angel Dust Apocalypse* (the short also made a later appearance in Issue #16 of Verbicide Magazine). I'd created this weird, paranoid guy with a fantastic suit made of roaches, I had him merc the President, and then I called it quits. But I always wondered, "What the hell would the guy do next?"

You're holding the answer to that question. How I got from that very economical short story to this absurd existentialist adventure, I honestly have no idea. I do know that I listened to only two albums during the entire process of writing the book: Bjork's *Vespertine* and DJ Dieselboy's *The Dungeonmaster's Guide*. Just those two, alternating, over and over again. And strangely, there is a pattern in the book, too, of moments of lightness countered by more brutal, frantic passages. I think the soundtrack had something to do with that.

Do you need to have read the aforementioned short story to appreciate this book? Nope. I tried as best I could to bring in enough details from the prior piece to make this a stand-alone tale. Would reading that story make this book a richer experience? Potentially. Both stories are now lodged so firmly in my skull that I can't separate them to venture a guess.

It's probably obvious by now that I am utterly obsessed with the end of the world via nuclear means. It's a fear that- even through the writing of these stories- I can't quite shake. If the big time bombs really did drop it would be such a fucking mess, and such a huge manifestation of disgusting human ego and power. I was discussing the end of the world with a friend of mine- one who happens to be a bio-chemist and recently invented a new virus, which although unrelated, is just really cool- and we both agreed that a broad pandemic is a much preferred form of mass human destruction.

Let nature take us out, if we have to go. Bombs are so tacky.

On a different, less End Times-y note, THANK YOU for supporting underground literature and picking up this title from Swallowdown Press. We don't exist without wonderful dedicated readers like you.

I think this book marks the end of Dean's adventures. Things in his world have become so strange that if I ever returned to his story I have a feeling things might turn out really, really weird.

God forbid, right?

Portland, OR, April '06

About the Author

Jeremy Robert Johnson is the Bizarro author of the cult hit *Angel Dust Apocalypse* and the Bram Stoker Nominated novel *Siren Promised* (w/Alan M. Clark). His fiction has been published in numerous magazines and anthologies. He is hard at work on two new books, *Tuning Fork* and *Skullcrack City*.

He currently resides in Portland, Oregon where he spends most of his time reading, writing, running, and enjoying the splendors of hybrid movie theater breweries.

For more information, spelunking maps, blog access, and news on upcoming projects check out:

www.jeremyrobertjohnson.com

Artist's Bio

Marie Peters-Rimpot, 41, was born and raised in Bretagne, France. She moved to the Netherlands when she was 22 and has lived there since as a mother to three wonderful children and as a respected self-taught artist. Her work is the result of a constant urge to create, whether the method is photography, short stories, sculpture, or digital manipulations. She has been honored to exhibit her art in Levallois Perret and Amanlys. To see more of Marie's work you can visit: **http://web.mac.com/marie.peters/iWeb/Marie/Home.html**

Siren
Promised

Jeremy Robert Johnson

Alan M. Clark

Siren Promised

Angie Smith and Curtis Loew are having dreams they can't shake. At the heart of each is Angie's daughter, Kaya. Angie's dreams end in death, the spreading of hand-shaped bruises across her daughter's throat. Curtis' dreams end in something else, something closer to obsession than love.

Angie is worlds away, trying to keep her drug-shattered mind from falling apart, traveling through an American underbelly filled with inhuman shapes, dark whispers and old friends with empty eyes.

Curtis is Kaya's new neighbor. He's getting closer to her, and her mentally unstable grandmother, Colleen. He's had families before, but he'd always made mistakes. Mistakes that led to new names, new towns. But this one time, he swears, things will all work out. He's got so much love to give.

Featuring an introduction from author Simon Clark, over thirty illustrations by Alan M. Clark and an afterword by the book's creators, the Bram Stoker Award nominated novel *Siren Promised* sets a new benchmark in visual and written storytelling.

"Using Alan M. Clark's gorgeously dark fantastique artwork to springboard the lush, compelling, often raw storyline forward, Johnson and Clark have created a unique literary atmosphere full of dread and wonder. This is a synergistic fusion of major talents that seethes with the black, beautiful energy of nightmares made real."- Tom Piccirilli, author of *Headstone City* and *A Choir of Ill Children*

ANGEL DUST
APOCALYPSE

JEREMY ROBERT JOHNSON

Angel Dust Apocalypse

Meth-heads, man-made monsters, and murderous Neo-Nazis. Blissed out club kids dying at the speed of sound. The un-dead and the very soon-to-be-dead. They're all here, trying to claw their way free.

From the radioactive streets of a war-scarred future, where the nuclear bombs have become self-aware, to the fallow fields of Nebraska where the kids are mainlining lightning bugs, this is a world both alien and intensely human. This is a place where self-discovery involves scalpels and horse tranquilizers; where the doctors are more doped-up than the patients; where obsessive-compulsive acid-freaks have unlocked the gateway to God and can't close the door.

This is not a safe place. You can turn back now, or you can head straight into the heart of... the *Angel Dust Apocalypse*.

"A dazzling writer. Seriously amazing short stories- and I love short stories. Like the best of Tobias Wolff. While I read them, they made time stand still. That's great."
- Chuck Palahniuk, author of *Fight Club*, *Choke* and *Haunted*

"[I]f you could marry well-crafted literature to stories of visceral horror, you would be holding *Angel Dust Apocalypse* in your hands. You'll laugh, you'll cry, you'll lose your lunch."
- Girl On Demand, *POD-dy Mouth*

Bizarro books

CATALOGUE – SPRING 2006

Bizarro Books publishes under the following imprints:

www.rawdogscreamingpress.com

www.eraserheadpress.com

www.afterbirthbooks.com

www.swallowdownpress.com

For all your Bizarro needs visit:

www.bizarrogenre.org

BB-001"**The Kafka Effekt**" D. Harlan Wilson - A collection of forty-four irreal short stories loosely written in the vein of Franz Kafka, with more than a pinch of William S. Burroughs sprinkled on top. **211 pages $14**

BB-002 "**Satan Burger**" Carlton Mellick III - The cult novel that put Carlton Mellick III on the map ... Six punks get jobs at a fast food restaurant owned by the devil in a city violently overpopulated by surreal alien cultures. **236 pages $14**

BB-003 "**Some Things Are Better Left Unplugged**" Vincent Sakwoski - Join The Man and his Nemesis, the obese tabby, for a nightmare roller coaster ride into this postmodern fantasy. **152 pages $10**

BB-004 "**Shall We Gather At the Garden?**" Kevin L Donihe - Donihe's Debut novel. Midgets take over the world, The Church of Lionel Richie vs. The Church of the Byrds, plant porn and more! **244 pages $14**

BB-005 "**Razor Wire Pubic Hair**" Carlton Mellick III - A genderless humandildo is purchased by a razor dominatrix and brought into her nightmarish world of bizarre sex and mutilation. **176 pages $11**

BB-006 "**Stranger on the Loose**" D. Harlan Wilson - The fiction of Wilson's 2nd collection is planted in the soil of normalcy, but what grows out of that soil is a dark, witty, otherworldly jungle... **228 pages $14**

BB-007 "**The Baby Jesus Butt Plug**" Carlton Mellick III - Using clones of the Baby Jesus for anal sex will be the hip sex fetish of the future. **92 pages $10**

BB-008 "**Fishyfleshed**" Carlton Mellick III - The world of the past is an illogical flatland lacking in dimension and color, a sick-scape of crispy squid people wandering the desert for no apparent reason. **260 pages $14**

BB-009 **"Dead Bitch Army"** Andre Duza - Step into a world filled with racist teenagers, cannibals, 100 warped Uncle Sams, automobiles with razor-sharp teeth, living graffiti, and a pissed-off zombie bitch out for revenge. **344 pages $16**

BB-010 **"The Menstruating Mall"** Carlton Mellick III *"The Breakfast Club* meets *Chopping Mall* as directed by David Lynch."* - Brian Keene **212 pages $12**

BB-011 **"Angel Dust Apocalypse"** Jeremy Robert Johnson - Meth-heads, manmade monsters, and murderous Neo-Nazis. "Seriously amazing short stories..." - Chuck Palahniuk, author of *Fight Club* **184 pages $11**

BB-012 **"Ocean of Lard"** Kevin L Donihe / Carlton Mellick III - A parody of those old Choose Your Own Adventure kid's books about some very odd pirates sailing on a sea made of animal fat. **176 pages $12**

BB-013 **"Last Burn in Hell"** John Edward Lawson - From his lurid angst-affair with a lesbian music diva to his ascendance as unlikely pop icon the one constant for Kenrick Brimley, official state prison gigolo, is he's got no clue what he's doing. **172 pages $14**

BB-014 **"Tangerinephant"** Kevin Dole 2 - TV-obsessed aliens have abducted Michael Tangerinephant in this bizarre combination of science fiction, satire, and surrealism. **164 pages $11**

BB-015 **"Foop!"** Chris Genoa - Strange happenings are going on at Dactyl, Inc, the world's first and only time travel tourism company.
"A surreal pie in the face!" - Christopher Moore **300 pages $14**

BB-016 **"Spider Pie"** Alyssa Sturgill - A one-way trip down a rabbit hole inhabited by sexual deviants and friendly monsters, fairytale beginnings and hideous endings. **104 pages $11**

BB-017 "The Unauthorized Woman" Efrem Emerson - Enter the world of the inner freak, a landscape populated by the pre-dead and morticioners, by cockroaches and 300-lb robots. **104 pages $11**

BB-018 "Fugue XXIX" Forrest Aguirre - Tales from the fringe of speculative literary fiction where innovative minds dream up the future's uncharted territories while mining forgotten treasures of the past. **220 pages $16**

BB-019 "Pocket Full of Loose Razorblades" John Edward Lawson - A collection of dark bizarro stories. From a giant rectum to a foot-fungus factory to a girl with a biforked tongue. **190 pages $13**

BB-020 "Punk Land" Carlton Mellick III - In the punk version of Heaven, the anarchist utopia is threatened by corporate fascism and only Goblin, Mortician's sperm, and a blue-mohawked female assassin named Shark Girl can stop them. **284 pages $15**

BB-021 "Pseudo-City" D. Harlan Wilson - Pseudo-City exposes what waits in the bathroom stall, under the manhole cover and in the corporate boardroom, all in a way that can only be described as mind-bogglingly irreal. **220 pages $16**

BB-022 "Kafka's Uncle and Other Strange Tales" Bruce Taylor - Anslenot and his giant tarantula (tormentor? fri-end?) wander a desecrated world in this novel and collection of stories from Mr. Magic Realism Himself. **348 pages $17**

BB-023 "Sex and Death In Television Town" Carlton Mellick III - In the old west, a gang of hermaphrodite gunslingers take refuge from a demon plague in Telos: a town where its citizens have televisions instead of heads. **184 pages $12**

BB-024 "It Came From Below The Belt" Bradley Sands - What can Grover Goldstein do when his severed, sentient penis forces him to return to high school and help it win the presidential election? **204 pages $13**

BB-025 "Sick: An Anthology of Illness" John Lawson, editor - These Sick stories are horrendous and hilarious dissections of creative minds on the scalpel's edge. **296 pages $16**

BB-026 "Tempting Disaster" John Lawson, editor - A shocking and alluring anthology from the fringe that examines our culture's obsession with taboos. **260 pages $16**

BB-027 "Siren Promised" Jeremy Robert Johnson - Nominated for the Bram Stoker Award. A potent mix of bad drugs, bad dreams, brutal bad guys, and surreal/incredible art by Alan M. Clark. **190 pages $13**

BB-028 "Chemical Gardens" Gina Ranalli - Ro and punk band *Green is the Enemy* find Kreepkins, a surfer-dude warlock, a vengeful demon, and a Metal Priestess in their way as they try to escape an underground nightmare. **188 pages $13**

BB-029 "Jesus Freaks" Andre Duza For God so loved the world that he gave his only two begotten sons... and a few million zombies. **400 pages $16**

BB-030 "Grape City" Kevin L. Donihe - More Donihe-style comedic bizarro about a demon named Charles who is forced to work a minimum wage job on Earth after Hell goes out of business. **108 pages $10**

BB-031 "Sea of the Patchwork Cats" Carlton Mellick III - A quiet dreamlike tale set in the ashes of the human race. For Mellick enthusiasts who also adore *The Twilight Zone*. **112 pages $10**

BB-032 "Extinction Journals" Jeremy Robert Johnson 104 pages - An uncanny voyage across a newly nuclear America where one man must confront the problems associated with loneliness, insane dieties, radiation, love, and an ever-evolving cockroach suit with a mind of its own. **104 pages $10**

BB-033 "Meat Puppet Cabaret" Steve Beard At last! The secret connection between Jack the Ripper and Princess Diana's death revealed! **240 pages $16 / $30**

BB-034 "The Greatest Fucking Moment in Sports" Kevin L. Donihe - In the tradition of the surreal anti-sitcom *Get A Life* comes a tale of triumph and agape love from the master of comedic bizarro. **108 pages $10**

BB-035 "The Troublesome Amputee" John Edward Lawson - Disturbing verse from a man who truly believes nothing is sacred and intends to prove it. **104 pages $9**

BB-036 "Deity" Vic Mudd God (who doesn't like to be called "God") comes down to a typical, suburban, Ohio family for a little vacation—but it doesn't turn out to be as relaxing as He had hoped it would be... **168 pages $12**

BB-037 "The Haunted Vagina" Carlton Mellick III - It's difficult to love a woman whose vagina is a gateway to the world of the dead. **132 pages $10**

BB-038 "Tales from the Vinegar Wasteland" Ray Fracalossy - Witness: a man is slowly losing his face, a neighbor who periodically screams out for no apparent reason, and a house with a room that doesn't actually exist. **240 pages $14**

BB-039 "Suicide Girls in the Afterlife" Gina Ranalli - After Pogue commits suicide, she unexpectedly finds herself an unwilling "guest" at a hotel in the Afterlife, where she meets a group of bizarre characters, including a goth Satan, a hippie Jesus, and an alien-human hybrid. **100 pages $9**

BB-040 "And Your Point Is?" Steve Aylett - In this follow-up to LINT multiple authors provide critical commentary and essays about Jeff Lint's mind-bending literature. **104 pages $11**

BB-041 "Not Quite One of the Boys" Vincent Sakowski -While drug-dealer Maxi drinks with Dante in purgatory, God and Satan play a little tri-level chess and do a little bargaining over his business partner, Vinnie, who is still left on earth. **220 pages $14**

COMING SOON:

"Misadventures in a Thumbnail Universe" by Vincent Sakowski

"House of Houses" by Kevin Donihe

"War Slut" by Carlton Mellick III

ORDER FORM

TITLES	QTY	PRICE	TOTAL
Shipping costs (see below)			
TOTAL			

Please make checks and moneyorders payable to ROSE O'KEEFE / BIZARRO BOOKS in U.S. funds only. Please don't send bad checks! Allow 2-6 weeks for delivery. International orders may take longer. If you'd like to pay online via PAYPAL.COM, send payments to publisher@eraserheadpress.com.

SHIPPING: US ORDERS - $2 for the first book, $1 for each additional book. For priority shipping, add an additional $4. INT'L ORDERS - $5 for the first book, $3 for each additional book. Add an additional $5 per book for global priority shipping.

Send payment to:

BIZARRO BOOKS
C/O Rose O'Keefe
205 NE Bryant
Portland, OR 97211

Address

City   State   Zip

Email   Phone

CPSIA information can be obtained at www.ICGtesting.com
Printed in the USA
BVOW08s2323270516

449478BV00002B/71/P